Rush

Of

Many

Waters

Also by Pauly Hart

Novels:
By the Gates of the Garden of Eden
Novellas:
Superior Respondent
Ouesso to Epena
The Book of Lesser Voices
Mountain to Mountain
The Word of Yahweh unto Enoch
Empire of the Dragon
Finance:
The Richest Man In Babylon Continued Stories
Collections:
Sometimes I Write Tiny Stories
Adelphoi
Poetry:
Stupid Mind Tricks
Book of Love and Laughter
The Cross and the Poet
What is Poep?
I Love You More Than a Fox Loves Blueberries
The Night Clerk Held a Broken Pencil
Spontaneous Psalms
Kick the Prick
Exegesis with Co-Authors:
My Flat Earth
Biblical Cosmology, 8+ languages
Translations:
The Testament of Job in Modern English
Children's:
Mathmagician and Other Tales of Awesomeness
Periodicals:
Modern Epistle (1-8)
Microzine (1-5)
Rush of Many Waters (1-20)
With children authors:
Farrell Family Fables
With Co-Author Jennifer Hart:
Adulting: A Daily Guide on Being an Adultier Adult
Audiobooks:
Biblical Cosmology
Superior Respondent

Rush of Many Waters:

Volume Five

By Pauly Hart

ISBN: 978-1-955399-09-8
Library of Congress Catalog Data is available at: Loc.gov
This book is available at cost on Amazon.com and wherever
fine books are sold.
Any references to historical events, real people, or real
places are used fictitiously. Names, characters, and
places are products of the author's imagination.
Front Cover Art by Franz Marc:
Front cover design by Pauly Hart
Paperback version printed in Savannah, Georgia, USA,
where available.
First Edition, 2021
Author Contact: EmpiresAndGenerals@gmail.com
Author Website: PaulyHart.com

Contents

Shorts

The Book of Lesser Voices

Andrews picks up a book and starts to read. The last asshole wouldn't miss the book. He had sucked his dick long and hard and had left him passed out on the dirty bed. Sometimes he lay with them, but he was hungry, so he had taken the money left on the counter, and the book next to it. What the hell. Maybe he wouldn't miss it. It was an old book and pretty beat up. On the front cover were words that he couldn't make out. He had thirty bucks. Two plain Mcdoubles and a glass of water. Seven bucks. Fuck McDonalds. They had changed the price of their value meal now, after they had taken away the extra piece of cheese a couple of years ago. *Something wrong with those fuckers*. He thought. The avenue was bright across the street from the motel. He sat outside in their meal area and watched the cars go by and opened up the book. In the front cover are the words: A Tale of Telling Choices. Fuck, this was old... And probably valuable too. People were looking at him. He hated people. He took his lunch to the alley behind the restaurant. There, in the light of the garbage flood-lamp, and the ever present drive thru customer, he took a bite and began to read.

It is about a girl named Bellatrix, named after one of the bright star in Orion's Constellation. Bellatrix is very upset about this. Some of the pictures call Orion the man with the shield and sword, some of them show him on one knee with a cyclops head, but she likes the one where he has a bow and arrow shooting a dragon. Some have him looking left, some have him looking right, but he should look at the dragon while he kills him she thinks. None of this matters to her much, it is only when people bring it up that she likes to have an informed opinion. She lives at her father's estate in Milton-under-Wychwood, but he is never there, and she has the run of the place. She opened a book called The Story of Shutting Doors.

It is about a young man traveling in Europe named Carl. He had heard of a terribly haunted forest named the Hoia Baciu Forest and had decided to go there and take some photos. He had a friend, Afina that lived in Romania, where the forest was and had gone to Babes-Bolyai University in Cluj-Napoca that skirted the northwest corner of the University. She had offered to show Carl around if he ever decided to visit her. They had dated, but that had been when she lived in the states. She had been attending Tulsa University, and he had been visiting his cousin there in "T-Town". They had met at a concert at a local bar on Cherry Street and they had a magical three weeks together. She had given him a book called <u>A Vale of Whispering Voices.</u> He had never read it, but brought it with him, to read on the way to meet her.

The story began with a young girl named Delsye, who lived in the Caribbean. It told her story. A girl in love with horses and races. Every morning at 4:30 she would get up and work with them. Her whole life had been with them. She lived on St. Croix Island in the United States Virgin Islands, by the airport, but every summer, her aunt would have her up to St. Johns. Her aunt, Lizbeth lived at the end of Marina Drive by Cololoba Cay and every morning she and Delsye would take the horses riding, and in some instances, swimming out over to Parrot or Genti Bay.

Carl slammed the book. It was too much. The scenery from the train ride was much better to look at.

Bellatrix thought that was odd, put the book down, wandering into the kitchen for a nice breakfast.

A cop shined his light at Andrew. "Time to move on kid. They don't like you hanging out back here." Andrew put his cigarette out, shut the book, and got up. "Sure man, whatever." He said. He walked away, leaving the cop shouting something about getting a job. He didn't care. Stupid pigs, they would get what they deserved. He did know one cop who wasn't that horrible. Maybe there might be one or two in the whole world but the rest of them sucked. Two years ago when he was first homeless and trying to find a job he had made it to Seattle by the "Gas, Grass or Ass" rule - mostly ass. He had sucked two truckers and finger banged some weird dyke in a station wagon to get there. It was similar to where he had lived in Bay City, Michigan; It was just bigger and meaner. It didn't rain all the time here, which is what he thought when he had first heard of it, but it did rain some. And it wasn't as cold as Michigan, by a long shot. Screw Michigan.

He had wanted to hit the road and live somewhere nice and safe and get a job and provide for himself. Then he had met Jeff Faster. The guy smoked him out on some good home-grown Sativa and they wound up spending a couple of weeks together smoking everything in sight until Jeff had taken his backpack in the middle of the night, leaving him with nothing.

That was the shittiest thing in the world. He had tried to find Jeff, but all of his friends suddenly didn't know where he was. They sucked too. Everything sucked. He had gone to the homeless shelter and heard about "Jesus who took away the sins of the world" every night, but it was free food and a hot cot. Days turned into weeks and he hung out with whoever would help him... And whoever would pay him to give them head. Then he had his first hit of Meth and the world turned gray.

Meth had become the greatest thing in the world. It still was. When he was tweaking - everything was faster, better, lighter. He was stronger, more agile, quicker, faster and... better. Can you be quicker and faster at the same time? He was faster than Jeff Faster, for sure. But it didn't matter. Ah. Meth, you sly little bitch. He should stop though. He smoked it and snorted it, but mostly drank it. Crystal (or Meth or Crank or whatever you wanted to call it) and sex. Sex and Crystal. He had become what they called a "Bag Fag"... Someone who just got amped in exchange for sex. But when he was up, he didn't care if it was Dick Dope or Biker Speed, he was a Nympho.

And right now, it was time to go score.

Carl ordered the sandwich and a Coke. Pastrami and Swiss on rye. Gross really. Stale lettuce and a slimy tomato just embarrassed the train service. They could have done so much better with their selection than to serve him this garbage. It was pathetic and he picked at it until their stop. Here he was at last, at the destination of his journey. He had come in from Budapest, from the west, and he had thought that he would have a view of the forest from his train, and he guess he had, but the countryside was splendid in every direction, so he couldn't tell if he had seen it or not.

Debark. He already had his luggage. Not much really, just his backpack that had been with him since Boy Scouts, but it held everything he needed. He was off. Mostly people his own age, some hotties and some notties. That was all good. He had a girl and he was alright with waiting to see her. The bulge in his pants proved him right. Adjusting his pack, his sweatshirt and discreetly, his bulge, he turned around looking for a map. His translator app on his phone helped him fumble thru: "Where is the university?" But it didn't matter. He should have just followed everyone. That seemed to be where people were going. Well... People were going everywhere really.

This place was crazy. Five lanes with pedestrian medians. Huge buses zipping down the streets sparking the off of the power lines that zig-zagged every which way. People crossing, mopeds zipping in between the cars that were dodging everything... And not a traffic signal in sight. Insanity. He smiled to himself and checked the signs. "Polus Center". Alright, seemed promising. Actually... Nothing seemed promising. He pulled up a map and got better bearings. He would figure this thing out yet.

It was Thursday. 3:30pm local time. He had wanted to surprise her. Afina loved old books, hated tech and had a passion for fresh baked bread. She would have thrown that train sandwich out of the window. She was Romanian alright. A wild girl with life to live and no apologies to give. The cars swooshed past and pedestrians weaved around him. The apartments all looked the same. Drab old brownstones with a courtyard here and there. The cars were all tiny and the people were mostly happy. This was going to be a good day, he decided. Nothing could hold him down.

"Dearest! I'm home!" came a call from downstairs. Father was home! Bellatrix left the book there on the floor where she had been reading and raced down the hallway. Nothing was a good day like when Father comes home. Bulgaria, or wherever. She thought Carl was boring and silly.

"I'm home honey!" Her father called again. "I'm here! She said, racing from her room out into the main hall. "I've brought Bangers and Mash from Mrs. McDougan's house!" He called as she heard him walk down the hall and into the kitchen.

Plop! Her stocking feet hit the main floor and raced around the corner to catch up to him. "Father! Father! What took you so long? It was dreadful waiting for you!"

He placed down the wicker basket on the counter just in time for her to reach him and tackle his legs. "Careful there pumpkin! I'm not going anywhere. Here. Let's set this table and we can eat to our hearts content and you can tell me all about your day."

He spat across the room and hit an old blanket. Sweet Jesus, this was terrible. Who the hell talks like that? Andrews folded the corner of the book over and looked at the inside flap again. Usually there was some sort of header or whatever. A list of things like the publisher or the date? Nothing. Just the title page that had the name and then the next page was the story. Not even the author. Fucking weird was what this was. Damn thing. He looked around the room.

In the corner was Dallas, his part time drug buddy. Dallas had let him use this house before but he wasn't about to stay the night here again. Dallas had some fucked up tweakers coming in and out at all hours of the night all the fucking time and Andrews just wanted to sleep. Just sleep. He had scored off Dallas around three hours ago and they had both passed out after the heroine high. It was that black tar shit that he hated so much but it was better than nothing. Some crack would have been nice, but Andrews didn't have enough for an eight ball and he missed heroine... He had run into Dallas after he left Micky-Dees and one thing led to another.

He got his bag and shook off the bread crumbs. Bread crumbs? Oh yeah, they had scored two loaves of some janky leftover Blue Bunny whole grain white bread and had a fight with it earlier before Dallas had talked him into a hand job. Dallas wasn't a faggot - he liked to look at magazines when Andrews jerked him off, but, hey free black was free black after all. Hand jobs were easy.

Asleep in the corner, Dallas didn't even notice Andrews leave.

It was a little after five in the afternoon according to the way the barge moved across the water. Delsye was told that it carried diesel fuel to Cruz bay from Christiansted. The water was cool today but not terrible. She waded in. The water was warm. It was nice and warm. She decided that she didn't need her suit. A quick dip in the blue was all she needed to feel right. She ran up and shook off her shorts and shirt up where the trees met the sand and ran back into the surf. It was nice. She was an expert skin diver, so her father had told her. Her mother didn't live with them anymore. She was from the T&T, Trinidad and Tobago, and had moved back there to be with her family. Delsye had cried for weeks but her mother hadn't cared. She had left and that was that.

Her mother was callous and cruel, Delsye knew and that was the end of that. Her father's sister, Lizbeth had told her father that she would do all she could to care for her and Delsye enjoyed spending time with her aunt. As much time as she could get. She looked below her. The fire coral danced and waved along with the waves, like the palms on the island. There was an eel slithering around. She wished she would have brought her harpoon with her, but she had left it at home. It was a small device, a stick and some surgical tubing, but she was a good shot. She decided to go and say hello to it anyway.

Down, down, down, stop. The eel had seen her and was darting away. *Zip!* It was gone. But it was pretty. One day she would catch one with her bare hands and wrestle it to the shore. But not today. Time for air. Up and up and breathe. No one in sight. An outrigger was on the horizon, but she didn't think anything of it. The barge was pulling around the bend and she could barely hear the *chug chug chug*. It would be gone soon. She went down again. Down, down, down, stop to the bottom. There, nothing bothered her. There on the floor, her mom and dad still lived together, there on the bottom, everything was alright.

In the ocean, everything was pristine. It had been a good day to dive after all. The surf was just right, not yet pulling outwards enough to muck up the bottom of the floor. She was thirty feet down, at her limit. She wanted to push herself every day to get a deeper and deeper depth, to get a longer time with each dive, and she would. The sea was good and pure and it would allow her to fall in love with it, dive by dive.

A Conch! Two! Three of them right beside each other! Awesome! She would catch them and bring them home to her aunt! Conch soup was one of her aunt's favorites, along with Macaroni and Cheese. Both, a delicacy in the Virgin Islands. She scooped one up, the other, and popping a finger in the shell of the third, she went back to the surface, the three conch's nuzzling her hands with their soft skin that came out of their shell, begging her to let them go. Not a chance.

She surfaced. Breathe! Air. Delicious air flooded her lungs. Kicking her legs was all the propulsion she would get now. Facing shore she began the long process of getting back in without losing her precious cargo. There was a splashing behind her. The outrigger was coming up on her, intent on landing on the beach. It was large, a Trimaran.

He looked up from the book and closed it. Delsye could wait. Right now Afina's classes should be done by now, but where was she? She had emailed him a list of her classes. He was outside of the right building all right. It was a little after two and unless she had decided to stay late, she should be out by... There! In a sky blue chamois and skinny jeans, her hair up in a pony-tail, she came bounding out of the building. She was breath-taking. Dark and lanky, and beautiful as hell. He got his backpack and stood up. She was excited and running. Had she seen him? Wait, she was running toward someone else... A man? A man. Light brown leather coat, long black hair and round glasses. She jumped into his arms and they kissed, deep and passionate. He scooped her up, she screamed, he spanked her ass and loaded her into a Jeep and they drove away.

"Oh stupid Carl." she said to herself as she lay on her bed. "Poor stupid Carl." She thumped it shut, placing it on her nightstand. All that work to go see her and she already has a boy. Poor stupid Carl. She adjusted the covers around her feet. Nothing was worse than cold toes. Cold toes were the worst thing in the world. Appolonia had come in sometime during the day and turned down the sheets. She was a very good maid, and Bellatrix had told her father that more than once.

Appolonia had only worked for them for three months. Bellatrix did not know where she was from, but she spoke with an accent. Not German, like old Ms. Fredrich, her tutor, but something foreign and delicious. "Oh goodness." she muttered to herself and drifted off to sleep She wondered what it would be like to grow up wherever Appolonia grew up. Was it far, far away? Did they have apple trees like they had here in England? Her father, away tomorrow in Gloucester, would not be able to tell her. She would ask Appolonia tomorrow.

But tomorrow never comes you little brat. Life sucks then you die.

He looked up at the ceiling. It was one of those popcorn jobs with little pieces of glitter. The pictures on the walls were those really nice but cheap replicas of ships at sea at dawn. The whole room was dressed in blue overtones and it was very chill.

Dallas had told him to stop by today. Blow-job this time. Nope. He was doing fine from a trick he had pulled for a suit in a Lexus. Shag time led to free smack and the suit had even paid for the hotel room. The suit wasn't into the drugs, just into him. He played catcher, and that was all good. He had been too fucked up to care. Damn. Good smack just makes it all worthwhile. It was ten in the morning and the front desk was calling. It had woke him up. He knew it was the front desk. No one ever called for him. The suit had left around one in the morning. They never stay.

"Late checkout please." He said in his most business like voice. The man on the other end was probably the husband or the uncle of the lady who had checked them in last night. Patel Hotels. They all had their relatives working and living there. Whites had been shoved out of the business a long time ago.

"Very well Mister Rogerson, our latest checkout is eleven thirty. Shall I have room service send up anything for you?" Fuck yes, he thought. "What's the special today?" He managed to not sound like a blabbering idiot. "Poached eggs, lightly smoked bacon, Nutella Crepes and fresh Italian espresso." His mouth watered. He had done this before and had fucked it up a couple of times and had found a foolproof way to get it done.

"Fine. Send that up. Add fifteen percent to the bill. I will be in the shower... Just put it in the room." he said like he was a suit himself. So pure. He should go into acting.

"Ah, we actually cannot add the tip to the bill without your signature. If you would like to sign the receipt at your checkout, we would be happy to have you sign it there," the desk jockey said in his Patel voice.

"Sure. Thanks." and hung up. Asshole. At least he would eat for free. He wouldn't sign anything. He wouldn't even walk out the front door. He would shower now, with all his stuff in the bathroom, eat after the room service left, wash his clothes and be out by 11:00. Those little hair dryers did a pretty good job of drying out clothes. He might even leave the hair dryer here this time.

Nah. Cause, hey... Free hair dryer.

Delsye had dropped the shells. They were almost on her, in the sleek Trimaran. Three scary dark skinned men. Screaming at her in Spanish. Probably Cubans, she thought. Her aunt had warned her about those kinds. Not Cubans, but men who only wanted her body. She said to stay away from them. Delsye was light skinned, tall, thin, and very pretty. Her aunt had said that she would have a problem with boys if she wasn't careful. But these weren't boys. These were men and they were fast. They were telling her to get in the boat. Telling her that there was nothing wrong with getting in the boat. That they wanted to touch her. That they wanted to do things to her.

She dove down. The floor was only six or seven feet here. She did what she thought would be best - she swam with all her might back out to sea. She was around fifty feet from the shore and she would have never made it all the way. Looking up, she was under the Trimaran. It's dirty white hull casting a shadow above her. Dark blobs that were men were on the side looking down. She would swim as fast as she could and get away. She didn't care if she had to run home without her clothes. She knew a way that she could get home pretty quick without being seen.

The Trimaran was turning. *Splash!* A diver had come in on top of her. No! No! No! Rough hands on her stomach and shoulders and things went dark.

Holy shit, Carl wondered how this chick was going to make it. She had left all her clothes on the shore. How old was she? Like twelve? It was only a book, but it made him feel really uncomfortable about it all. Why had Afina given him the book to begin with? Where was she anyway?

He had watched the prick (that was his name for the hipster that had kissed her) drive them both out and away from the university. That was an hour ago. He had no idea what he was going to do with himself so he had walked to her flat and waited. He didn't want to flip out but he didn't want the prick to see him either. He would just wait until she was dropped off and then ring her doorbell and act like he just got there. But he wanted to do it alone.

Delsye awoke to darkness. It was cold and she was curled up in a ball. She tried to stretch, but she was in a box. Pushing with all her might was a mistake, a huge knot cramped up in her leg and squeezed until she screamed. *Bam! Bam!* Came the loudest sound she had ever heard.

"Callate perra!" came the shout from up above. *Bam!* Again the metal box echoed the sound to her bones. The cramp burned its way into her mind and she grit her teeth. She tried pushing this way and that and it wouldn't let go of her. She grabbed at it, pushing the muscles back down, and still it wouldn't budge.

"Ahhhhhaaaaa." came the whine through her teeth. She sucked in air slow and long and tried not to cry, but the tears came anyway.

Eventually the slow rocking of the boat and the fear drove her back to unconsciousness. Was it sleep? She didn't know, but the next time she woke up, she had wet herself. Her head was sideways on the floor and the urine rushed into her mouth and nose, stinging her.

"Gah!" She screamed, and jerked up, spitting. The acrid taste burned. She cried to be let out. It got their attention. The men undid the lid slowly. Their black shapes outlined the starry night.

Carl had waited for hours in front of her flat only to grow cold and hungry. Several people would stop by and ask if he was alright. He didn't know enough Romanian to respond anyway so he kept silent and waved them on. Finally she had arrived. He had dropped her off and she had gone inside. She seemed angry about something. He waited five minutes until after he was gone before he got up, went over and knocked. He was nervous and had every right to be nervous. Why shouldn't he be nervous? He was being foolish maybe. Maybe. Maybe not. He knocked on the door.

"Party in the woods" read the flier Andrews held in his hand. "What part of the woods?" He said to himself and put the note back down on the cart. Another party. Another score maybe. He was out of the shower and the bellman had left the breakfast just like he'd asked him to. But there was a flyer on it. What the fuck was the dude thinking, leaving it on his breakfast cart? Who knew? Something to get him fired if Andrews had been legit probably. Didn't matter. The breakfast was awesome and he thought about it as he used the blow-dryer on his clothes. He only had the one set, so clean was better than dirty.

His pants took the longest and they were never all-the-way dry when he did this so he started them first with the t-shirt hanging on a hanger to catch the draft. The fan was on and he was finished drying both pretty quickly. The dryer was one of those bolted down jobs so he couldn't score that. There was nothing really to take except maybe a towel. And they were nice towels. So boom, one towel went into his bag. He was ready to go. Party in the woods got crumpled and stuffed into his pocket along with his knife and the money he had scored. He didn't have a wallet anymore since his encounter with Jeff. That fucking scum. Thanks Jeff. He opened the door and looked both ways before walking to the stair-case.

"Get up." The voice said to her. It was English this time, not Spanish but she was still scared. "Put these on." Some clothes were thrown at her. Not her clothes. She put on the dirty cut-off jeans and the t-shirt. "Rockin in STX - brought to you by the Mongoose" it said. She recognized it. The old white guy radio station from Saint Croix. She put it on slowly. She knew they were watching her. Were they Crucians? She had thought they were Cubans. It didn't matter. She was still scared out of her wits. She had heard about this. People kidnapped other people all the time. Would they touch her? She wondered if she would see her dad again.

"Where you live nah?" The same voice asked her. She didn't say anything. She was too afraid. The slow clap of the waves hit the hull. She didn't see lights on anywhere on the boat but knew they were still out to sea. She couldn't see shore either. "Me askin where you live!" The man shouted and hit her head with his palm. It didn't hurt but the words started pouring out.

"I live with my dad in Strawberry on St. Croix!" she screamed shaking. She loved her dad. "Please don't hurt him!"

"Gwaaan." Another voice said. "Whatcha doin out here nah? Gwan fishin for Conch on Johnny ain't nothin for a Crucian to be out for."

"She too young mon." Said the first voice to the other man, and then to her: "Whatcha doing on Johnny?" Saint John's, called "Johnny" by some of the islanders was typically for the rich.

"Imma stayin with my auntie." She got out. "She lives on Marina Drive"

"Oohhh" Said the second man. "That's right up the way. Maybe she pay somethin for da little fish we caught."

"Maybe she got money?" The first man said again. "She white?"

Delsye was light skinned black. Her father was light skinned but he was Crucian. He had some white in him from way back and people told her she looked like him.

"Nah, she's Tommyan." Meaning that she was from Saint Thomas, and also black.

"*Sssss.*" The first one sucked his teeth at her, disbelieving. "She gotta be white and marry a Carib to have a girl like you. She white and she you mom nah?" He didn't mean the Carib. He meant Caribbean-black. She told them again that it was her aunt, but they hit her again.

"Back in the box little fish or you tell us where she be." She knew she shouldn't tell them, but if she didn't they would stick her back in the box for sure. She didn't move.

"Right nah!" Cried the first. "Back in the box, fish!"

"Okay! Okay!" She was crying, and told them where her aunt lived.

Bellatrix had waited all day for her father who never came. Carl's story wasn't there but she kept reading into Delsye's story. How horrible. Was this even suitable for children? She wandered back down to her father's study to look at the spot where she had gotten it. Right... Right - there? No. She couldn't remember. Where had she gotten it from? The top shelf? Yes. She got the ladder from the side of the bookcase and scampered up. Not there either. There was a place for each book and even some dust. No books had been moved. Not the top shelf then.

Then where?

She squinted her eyes to remember. She couldn't. Appolonia would know. She went around to the conservatory to ask her but she wasn't there. She found her in the kitchen cleaning the stove.

"Miss Apples." Bellatrix called her. She loved calling her that.

"Yes young miss?" Appolonia brought her head up and around to look at her. A lock of her dark curly hair and a quick smile was what made her pretty. It wasn't the face. There was a long scar that ran from the left side of her neck to her ear and when she smiled, a strange dimple was made on that side of her face. But it was a beautiful smile anyway. Bellatrix loved her instantly then, if there had never been love there before, there was now.

"I was quite curious as to where the book came from," she said.

"And which book would that be?" Appolonia asked, the smile a little less bright.

"The book I've been reading about a college man traveling to one of those universities in eastern Europe. Romania of all the silly places to have a college. And then he is reading a story about a little negro girl who is kidnapped. It's all very terrible and sad and I don't know if I like it, but I want to read it now, just to see what happens." She was exasperated from the endeavor to hide her emotions about the girl and sat down next to Appolonia.

Miss Apples, as Bellatrix called her, put her brush down in the bucket, wiped her hands on her apron and also sat. She looked long and deep at Bellatrix in a way that would have scared her if it had been Ms. Fredrich, her tutor.

"But you are reading it. There is that." She said and looked away, wringing her hands. "I was never able to read it. It was too horrible when I owned it."

"Too horrible?" Bellatrix asked.

"Yes. And it was not about a college man or a girl that was kidnapped. It was about pirates and it was filled with a grim sadness that has never left me." She paused and looked again at Bellatrix. "It was given to me by a man, I guess you would call him my grandfather, and I have given it to you, to see what you would read."

"What do you mean - 'What I would read?' Isn't it the same book? How is it different for you?"

Appolonia paused and thought, biting the inside of her cheek as she thought, the pursing of her lips off to one side made Bellatrix think of a chipmunk. "When my grandfather read it, it was of the great 'Fourth Crusade', when the Catholics slaughtered the Christians at Byzantium. He could not read it 'without the world being crumpled' and gave it to me.

Bellatrix gave this some thought. Her eight year old brain chewed on the logic of this for a minute. A twelve year old would have dismissed this as idiotic or fantasy, but Bellatrix was not yet twelve, not yet in the category to dismiss the incredible. The blessing of being a child was that there was still a notion that all life was mystical and this was no different. Her life, blessed as it was, was not without the mystical category. That she was alone this summer, and her father had broken most promises of picnics and trips to the shore notwithstanding, she still had the one thing that all children who are still untainted share. A glimmer of hope for tomorrow.

Andrews cried late into the night, remembering his father killing himself. Walking into the house. The smell of burned hair. The wall that had been painted red by the shotgun blast. The empty body and later - the police.

They had thought Andrews had killed his father. He was thirteen and had hated his father with every fiber in his body. Little Andrews Steiner was suspect number one in the "Murder Investigation" as he would later find out. He remembers watching the interview later when they had detained him. They made him watch the interview again and again. The child psychologist had been the one to suggest it. But it was the pigs who had been so fucking mean about it.

"There. There you see that? You smiled. Why would you smile? You happy you killed him? Huh?" The detective harassed.

"Detective!" The psychologist had yelled. But it didn't make any difference. They laid into him again and again. But Andrews had continued smiling. He was happy the old man had bought his one way ticket. He hated him and was glad he was gone. There was nothing but the dull ache now, but in the video you could still see the smile underneath the shaggy black hair. The black hair that would be bleached white, then red, then back to black over the course of the year that he was remanded in the Juvenile Correctional Facility. When he turned fifteen, he had been 'adopted' by an emergency foster family, but that didn't last. He had gone from their care to into another home and then another, the next one worse than the last. It was a cycle that never ended and Andrews had left, or rather, run away at the third home.

"That's quite enough!" The psychologist had yelled. He was done with the Detectives bumbling around.

"Think about what I've said!" The detective slammed his fist down on the table with a loud whack. He straightened his tie, turned around a left the room. There was a silence. The psychologist had put his hand on Andrews' knee. He was thirteen years old.

He raised his head and rubbed out the familiar tears from the corner of his eyes. It was always the same. Those damned memories came back on him every night. Here it was again. He needed a fix.

Appolonia talked to Bellatrix late into the night. The stove could wait for another day. They had moved into the study where Bellatrix had found the book. Appolonia sat on the floor next to her with the book between them.

"Open the book child." she commanded. Bellatrix opened it to where she had last read, where the bookmark had been. The words were there. The same words that she had read earlier. "Now close it and open it again, this time without the bookmark. Open it like you would open it for the first time."

Bellatrix did as she was asked, and again, the book opened up to the same page. She tried again. It opened up to the same page again. She tried to flip backwards. She couldn't... Or rather, she could, but when she would try to leave it on that page, it would open back up to the page where she had left off. She was frightened. "It's all the same page!" her voice raised in frustration.

"Let me try." Appolonia said and took the book in her hands. She shut the front cover. She opened the book somewhere in the middle. The book was blank. Slowly, as if by some awkward effect, the page became inky and slowly, ink started swirling around and began to form letters.

Smack! Appolonia shut the book. "That's as far as I've ever let it get. I never let the cloud form any words. I don't want to be caught up in the spell. You open it to where I had it open now." She slid the book over to her. The book was flat on the floor. Bellatrix held her hand on the books cover... And opened it to the middle of the book. Except that it was the exact same page that she had left off reading. She stared in disbelief at the book and then again at Appolonia. There was no way.

"I cannot believe this!" She almost cried. "This is the same page as before."

"And yet it is not." Appolonia cautioned. "It is farther along in the book than you would like, yet it is not farther than you have read. Look at the next page. Actually, keep flipping the pages until you cannot flip them anymore."

"What? Like the end of the book?" Bellatrix questioned.

"No, just flip one or two at a time. Try not to read them, but instead, look at the floor, but be aware of the book in the corner of your eyes."

She did as she was she was asked. Each page seemed to be a copy of the last... Yet as she went, flip, the pages didn't seem, flip, to hold words anymore, flip, they had a face, flip, It was a man, flip, and he was holding a book, flip, and he was looking at her. Flip. It was Carl.

Carl jumped back. What the hell? He slammed the book and jumped off the bed. It clattered to the floor next to his backpack. The hotel room was tiny, but that was alright. Afina had suggested it. She had been shocked to see him at first, but relieved a little. She had said that she knew why Carl had come and that it would take some explaining to do, but the man she had been with was out the door, she had just needed the right reason. Carl didn't believe it, but she did hook him up with the super cheap room and promises of a meal and her company.

He went to the restroom. He had picked up the book again to kill time but there was no way that he had read what he read. He was watching a red haired girl from the fifties on the floor with a book and they had been reading about a man reading a book in a hotel room. Where the hell was Delsye? What was with this book? He washed his face. Getting a whiff of his underarms, he washed those with the washcloth as well. He went back into the bedroom and grabbed the book.

There was no author. Not in the front page, not on the spine. Red leather, gold script in an old font. "A Vale of Whispering Voices" it read. The title took the entire spine. It was thick. Almost like a ledger. Maybe around two hundred pages, dyed red on the outside, like an old bible, but not that crappy paper they used. Nice thick pulpy stuff, like the kind you use in children's books. And it was not what he expected. He shoved it in the bag.

It was almost time to meet Afina anyway. He wasn't a complete idiot and didn't want all his stuff taken when he was gone, so he got his backpack ready, threw it on, and almost opened the door. No. There was still thirty minutes left. Signing, he sat back down and opened the book.

Bullshit, thought Andrews. Buncha tweakers. This book was dumb as fuck, he thought, but curiosity got him again and he looked at the outside of the book. Red leather. Gold cursive. Red binding. Thick pages. "Huh." he said to himself.

"Huh?" said Dallas.

"Nothin man." Andrews said and shut the book. He would check it out later. Dallas had got the brown stuff this time. It was better than the black shit. Andrews pulled back his hair into a pony tail and undid Dallas's pants. "I'll tell you later."

But he never did.

Delsye had been taken to her aunt's house. The men had dragged her up the steps to the house and made her call her aunt to the door. Her aunt, God bless her, had resisted opening at first, but the men were quiet and angry and deadly. There they had raped her and her aunt. Each man, rougher than the last, had taken her on the kitchen table.

Delsye had never kissed a boy. She had never showed her parts to a boy. She was a good girl. They had tied her hands, and they had hurt her. She fought at first. She had tried. But it went on and on and she gave up. She threw up. They beat her. Darkness came and she was grateful.

It must have been near dawn when she came back. She had dreamed the whole thing. She had to have dreamed the whole thing. No. The men were drinking, playing dominoes in the kitchen. It was dawn. She was on the floor. There were arms around her. She didn't mean to, but she groaned when she turned to look at who it was. The men had heard her. Her aunt squeezed her tighter. "No child." she whispered.

"Ciete!" One of them swaggered in, pointing a machete and went back to the kitchen.

The house was the only house on the point. It was a concrete structure, painted an orange coral color and had stairs to the beach. Her aunt enjoyed canning. They both enjoyed reading. Her aunt only went to town once a week. No one would look for her here. No one would come, which is why it was a surprise to everyone when the banging came on the door.

Carl wants to read on, but the banging on the door should be Afina. And it is. With the man she swears is not her boyfriend. A man with dead eyes. "Gotfreid" he says, and puts his hand out. Carl shakes it and they leave. A picnic is in order, Afina tells him. They are going to the haunted forest next to the university. Everyone does it, it will be fun. He gives in and they begin their walk.

"No Carl... You silly man." Bellatrix scolds him. "Not with the man." she says, as she's propped up in bed.

Carl agrees. It's distasteful, but Afina brought him, how could he be rude and ask to go alone?

The men playing Dominoes are gasping, making wet wheezing noises, blood coming out of their holes. He has a gun? She saw them choking on their own blood. She hadn't heard any sounds of gunfire. He was bending over her now, questioning her. Her aunt was being lifted. Her aunt was dead. How had that happened? It seemed like she was watching everything thru a long corridor. There was her aunt. There she was, she looked at herself. At... The... Man... Was he even a man? His eyes met hers. Something about them. His hand reached out and picked her up as well. She would be safe now. She would be...

"Wait." Gotfreid said. "What do you mean it's blank?"

"Like I said." Carl said, showing him. "The rest of the book is blank. I'm not making this up." He passed the book over to Afina and Gotfreid. He thumbed thru it. From where Carl was, it appeared that the entire book was blank.

"How is it..." Carl began.

"Oh don't worry. These are always blank for me." Gotfreid smiled and handed the book to Afina, who sat between them. The pages swirled and danced with ink, not letters... A storm of black on white. She slammed it shut and handed it back to him.

"Would you like me to tell you what this book is?" she asked. Something in her voice told Carl that he should listen.

"Ye-yes." He said and listened to her as she told him.

"Ugh, Miss Apples, is she going to tell him the same thing that you told me last night?" Bellatrix had dressed and was reading at the table. A steaming pot of beans and freshly made toast were in front of her, but she hadn't eaten a bite.

"Probably." She slammed the book shut and placed it on the cutting table.

"Hey!" Exclaimed Bellatrix.

"You need to eat your breakfast first! Your father is coming home tonight, and we have a lot to do before he gets home."

"But Mrs. Fredrich is coming over soon." Bellatrix whined. "She won't let me read."

"I have sent word to the woman." Appolonia said. "She is not coming today. I have told her that you are sick."

"You told a lie?" Bellatrix gasped in disbelief.

"Yes. I told you we have a lot to do." Appolonia said. "And I've made you a Currant Pudding as well to take with us. Hurry! Eat your breakfast so we can leave!"

It is normally scary in the Wychwood, even in the middle of the day, yet today, for some reason, Bellatrix feels undaunted by the gray trees and dead grass. Even the pale yellow flowers that make her feel ever so dismal, are not bringing her down. She feels alive. When they had walked for almost an hour, Appolonia calls them to a halt. They spread out their blanket, have some biscuits and tea, and open the book. It is almost alive in her hands. The words are sharper, more defined somehow... The book feels powerful.

"It is this place." Appolonia points around her. "Forests hold the power for the books. There is a birthing place here for them. For they come from trees, and to the trees do they call. This very book was cut from this forest. When the book returns to its place of enchantment, it thins the veil between the other books.

You will notice that I did not say 'written' but rather: 'enchanted', for that is exactly what has been done to it, and you are the rightful bearer of the title. There are not many like you, dearest Bellatrix, but you are one of only a few, and I am quite sure that you will be able to talk to Carl here. Open the book." she said.

A pulling sensation began on his mind. Carl couldn't tell what it was, but he needed to read the book. Afina had talked about books and forests. Kalimsa? The Monks of Mayhem? The Order of the Vongonican. There was a lot that she had said that she had either just been pulling his chain on, or this whole thing was a lot deeper and weirder than he had ever believed. All he knew was, she could be full of complete shit.

Yet... The book swirled in her hands.

He picked it up and opened it.

Bellatrix was looking at Carl's face. There were no words. There was nothing there but Carl, just how she knew his face would be. Silly and dumb.

"I'm not dumb." Carl said to her. "I'm just confused. How the hell is this happening?"

"Oh my, what language!" Bellatrix chided. "Have you no courtesy in the presence of a lady?" she mocked. She was a brat and she knew it, but it was all in jest. Here was Carl and he would tell her that things would be alright... She hoped. Miss Apples had told her that is what would happen, and she trusted her.

"What's your name?" Carl asked. "I feel like I should know it, but I can't say it."

"Bellatrix, silly. You should have read it." She knew that he wouldn't have been able to, but she wanted to push him a little.

"Sorry." he apologized. "This is a little... weird. Talking to a book."

"Why are you dressed like that?" She asked. "Is it your bedtime?"

"What?" He asked. "No, these are just clothes."

"Well. Shouldn't a proper man dress with a tie?"

"Wait..." he said. "What year is it in this story?"

"Why Nineteen hundred and fifty two of course." She exclaimed. "What year do you think it is?"

"It's Nineteen ninety-eight here." He said slowly. They were both silent for a minute.

"What's your story like?" They both said at once. Bellatrix laughed and Carl laughed to. "You first." They both said at once again. They both laughed even harder.

"Alright Carl." Bellatrix went ahead. I am reading of you and your terrible decisions. Well... Truthfully it is actually quite awkward. I am reading of you reading of a girl. That poor girl. Whatever has happened to her? Your book is really blank?" She asked.

"Yes!" The truth of him knowing that she knew all about his book didn't phase him in the slightest, though he wondered why it didn't. "You know about what I've..." He began.

"Everything!" She exclaimed, a little too happily. "Did you know you snore?" she told him.

"Wait. You read that I snore? What's it like reading that? Did you see my dreams?"

"Not really. It's quick. Maybe a paragraph. Mostly that you snored a lot."

"But I don't know anything about you." Carl said. He was beginning to understand a little. "So. You are reading about me reading about Delsye. Who - or is there even... Is someone reading your story?"

"Miss Apples seems to think so." She said.

She had explained to him who Appolonia was, and he had explained to her who Afina was and that was the start of the feeling. Like a spider that you had known was coming down on top of your head, but you had just refused to acknowledge it, your brain, blocking it out somehow... It was a feeling of being watched. She felt it too.

He had known where they were. It had taken a little while to find out where to go to get to the girl, but once he had tuned in to her, it took just a little practice and he went to her.

He had killed the men first. They meant nothing to him. Then he had killed her aunt. Then her. And it wasn't long after that he found the others.

They had appeared at first as a flicker in his mind. And all it took was a walk into the forest and there they were, innocent and pure, talking about books. And he took them as well.

Killing the man and the girl had made his blood boil, his head rush, and gave him the hardest erection he had ever known.

The witches that were with them bound, closed and burned the books, making those portals shut forever... But that made little difference. He would hunt more and find more. This was a thousand times better than crystal meth or heroine, Andrews thought.

Poems

He is the son of man, come to seek and save the lost.
He is the son of God, my master, yes, the Christ.
He is the faithful and the true witness.
He is the Alpha and the Omega, the first to the end.
He is the bright and morning star.

He is the door of the sheep pen.
He is the good shepherd who would lay down his life.
He is the rhythm of the sea, the gateway to salvation
He is the one who forsook all to come and find us
He is my lover in a thousand ways.

He is in the Father and the Father is in him.
He is the works of the Father, The good steward.
He is Master, King, and Lord over all of creation.
He is the one who searches the heart, soul, and mind.
He is the great and mighty healer, the great physician.

He is the bread of life, he came so no one would hunger.
He is the manna from heaven. The fire and also the cloud.
He is the giver of eternal water and of all eternal life.
He is the life, the way, and the truth, the weary may come.
He is sweet sanctifier, servant, logos and rhema.

He is the light of the world. Take your cross and follow.
He is the life. He is the way. Keeper of Abrahams' bosom.
He is holy, faithful and true, He opens and no man shuts.
He is the true vine. He abides in the Father forever.
And we are his children, friends, sisters and brothers.

Dry tears

You left me naked
You left me alone
Vying for affection
And you give, give, give
Still you still stand there
With dry tears staining
Your fabric of life
Wide eyes trusting
Bright teeth smiling
You leave me helpless
I stand alone
Listening to yours
And I give, give, give
And I stand there
With hands a-folded
On my weary breast

Tired eyes closing
Dim smile fading
Won't you come to me?

Round and round

I tire of chasing you.
I have talked and have written,
Listened and conversed.
I have heard your dark secrets...
Don't you realize I like you?

Isn't this something like dating?
Yet you insist that you don't date...
I would like to know you better,
But you hide behind your walls.

Does my love fall dead at your feet?

The light behind your laughter...
The joy behind your eyes...
It's pain that makes you smile...
And tears have fed your songs.
Did you know I like your voice?

I know you but I don't.
I know you more than you like.
You want me to go away,
But complain when I don't write.

I'm looking for an explanation,
I'm looking for some kind of sign.
I'll come and take your hand,
If you will only take mine.

Barren Land

So here I stand in the wilderness
    of another place.
I stand this ground
    as a foreigner on strange soil.
But none have been meant
    to roam these lands as I.
It is their world, their place, their time.

The wind... I feel it breathing.
Whispering secrets of another mans home.
So here I am and here I stand (alone).
A foreigner in another mans land.

Earth, wind, rain and fire.
I hear the melody lifted higher.

I feel the wind and I feel the sand.
The remnant of this barren land.
I wish my dreams could become true.
Lord, let this land begin anew.

Someone.   Somewhere.

I was on the edge of anywhere
and I stood motionless before
a sea of tortuous thought and hate
seething, pulsing, breathing.
All I had to do was fish.
But I resisted the urge of death.
"Anywhere but anywhere", I cried out.
And He took my hand
and led me to a somewhere.

I'm just a no-one
trying to tell any-one
about a some-one
who loves every-one.

now blue

It has occurred to me to come to grips
With amazing things
I have believed in God to help me through
All my disbelief
Lord I see you in truth and your glory
Written on your wings
And now I walk by faith and not by sight
Give you everything
Today forsaken clean from all my sin
Now washed with joy true

Midnight treasures are gone, they were but rust
Now blue is now blue
Fragmented dangers fall covered in dust
Coming, gripping you
Nothing more can hold me, not one touch me
I will follow you

Flavor

My Vanilla
Drips
Forming White
Smudges
Plop It
Goes
And I
Grimace
But Also
Think
My Patience
Runs
Down My
Hand
But I
Wish
That I
Had
A Special
Flavor
For My
Shoes
To Go
With

Lord I want to love you more
Lord I want to love you more
Lord I want to love you more
Lord I want to love you more

Lord I want to serve you more
Lord I want to hold you more

And I want to praise you
From the top of my lungs
Cause I don't care if the police come

Hi come on in!
Would you like some doughnuts?
Or maybe some coffee?
Am I breaking a noise ordinance?

Not I don't think so
I'm just praising Jesus
Even if it's against the law
I do it till they nail me
Against the wall

I wont take the mark
I wont serve Mammon
But I'll serve only Messiah

All one solution:
To serve the Lord

Essays

Stories Jack Kirby Told

Not only did I burn all of my comics but I burned all of my role-playing games and my science fiction novels. I was saying goodbye to space, goodbye to extra-terrestrial aliens and goodbye to anything that would subvert the authority that God had placed in my life. Basically I had the idea that the throne of my heart was occupied with the idea of science and science-fiction and that had been a sin for me. To rid myself of those ideas and loves would free up the throne for God to take control. My dad and mother thought I had lost a wing-nut somewhere and that I was a little bonkers for doing it, but they helped me accomplish the task at hand. From what I remember, it took most of the day, but oh what a day it was.

It wasn't a grim task, and from I recall, it was hilarious for me to break those chains. I did have a little fun with it and tallied up the sticker prices of each comic before they met their fiery death. I had amassed over $3,000 in comics. Most of them today are worth that or a little more, because I had planned on holding on to them as an investment. I had many rares and first prints of some pretty valuable names and I won't bore you with the details, but I'm looking up prices right now and some of those are worth over $500. Oh well. "No Ragrats" as they say. The throne of my heart was worth more than all the art ever created. Seriously dude, I feel that way still today. With that bold statement to my family and the great story to tell later on (uh, you know, like right now), I gave God his rightful place inside my soul.

But it wasn't saying goodbye to fiction; it wasn't saying goodbye to great storytelling. I am still a fan of both of those. God created the mind for imagination, just not vain imaginations. I was saying goodbye to the idea that out there, somewhere in the multi-verse were powers that could battle with each other and maybe, luckily, the good guy would win and the earth would be averted from disaster yet another day. Thanks good guys. This came to a head in my mind when the Beyonder entered the Marvel Universe. Himself a mythic being from his own dimension, he only sought to be understood and Reed Richards killed him. The parable wasn't lost on me. I thought of Jesus Christ, infinitely more powerful than any Beyonder and yet we killed him on the cross.

But what was it about space and aliens that had so drew me? It was the quest for enlightenment. But it was a false path. There was only one way to salvation and I was shirking it and selling my heart out to Longshot, Donatello, and Mister Mxyzptlk. I had traded the truth of God for a lie and liked it. The more I distanced myself from these things in my heart, the more my heart yearned to find out what actually was the true power in the cosmos. What was the reality of God and Satan? Had the miracles I saw at Harvest Christian just a ruse? Was it all trickery and hypnosis? Or was there an actual God who still had his hand on the pulse of the world. I would later tell myself that this was the first step in becoming one of His disciples.

Now, I can't suggest that you go home and burn all of the things in your life that lead you away from God. I can't suggest that you literally take it outside and light it on fire. This was my solution. This was my declaration to the heavens that I was repenting of their false teachings and turning back to He who made me. A little severe for some, but, again, this is what I felt I must do. Much later in life, when I found myself sinning with TV, I would take it and put it on the curb. Again, a drastic solution to what could be a small problem. I once knew a man who quit smoking but kept a full pack of cigarettes on his coffee table to remind him where he had come from. I don't have that kind of willpower. When I am done with something, it goes away for good.

1986 would be the year I said goodbye to my belief in any real possibility of the solar system, the local group, the galaxy, the universe and the multiverse and trusted that God, who had created all, did so just like the Bible said He did.

And I will worship
(Thoughts inspired by Keith Wheeler)

I usually ache when I work. I sweat and grind and sputter away doing my endless tasks. I spend my time making money for those who take it away. I use what little I can to support my family who love me in return. The rest... well, the rest is gone. There is typically nothing left at the end of the check. This is the way it is with my God. I live my life for myself and for others, and when the time comes to give God his due, there is no time left. Perhaps I should re-evaluate my spent time. What could work out the best? I believe that if I turned over all of my firsts (all of my beginnings) to God, it could prove to be beneficial. If I give it up... will I get it back? I guess I am reminded of a certain promise: "No one has left father or mother or spouse in vain, they will receive back their due in this life and in the life to come.". Well it sure sounds nice doesn't it? What if I am to go whole-hog and embark on this teaching? will it turn out to work? Will it bring results? Yes. I believe that it will. If I open my heart out to the Lord each day before opening it up to anything else, day after day; and if I tithe the first part of my paycheck, instead of the leftovers... and if I really DO love God with all my heart and soul, then He will prove to be the God that He is destined to be in my life. He is Jehovah. The Boss. El Senior. I often wonder why we sing the song: "Oh magnify the Lord"? How can God actually get any bigger than what He already is? We also have heard the saying "More of You". How is it possible for us to have more of an omnipresent God in our life?

Perhaps it is the reverse of these two sayings in reality that is truth. We need to magnify our relationship with Him in our lives... and HE needs more of US. We must give God what is His, what is ours and even what we even think is ours. In truth, everything is His. How could we even claim that "I earned it with my own sweat and blood." Who do you think gave you the ability to work in the first place? Who gave you breath? Arms? Legs? Who gave you life? See, the Earth is the Lords and all that is in it. He made it and He owns it. He lets us live on His planet to do the things he has commanded. Love God and love people. That's about all we are summed up to do. As Adam was a Gardener and a Zoologist, and Jesus was a Carpenter, so we must work with all our might towards our calling on this planet. But like the two, we must always give firstfruits to the one who created us. That is why we, in the Western World pray before our meal instead of after. I must ask myself, that, in light of all this, what am I to do with my family and my spouse and everything that I deem "mine"? I believe that I will stick with Joshua on this one. "As for me and my house... we will serve the Lord".

A Man named Keith Wheeler

In 1994, in my third year of Seminary, my program director was Keith Wheeler. Keith was the most "In Love with Jesus" person that I had ever met. He challenged our little group of twelve to let go of "Modern American Churchianity" and to embrace the living Christ. This was a stark contrast to the program I had been in the year earlier where the program leader had prompted us to research and learn everything that we could about Church Polity to the betterment of the 501(c)3 enterprise... And to increase shareholder value... Something like that.

I had just gotten off of my wild ride the first two years at the school, learning how to run sound systems, understanding the envelope folding machine at the Data Processing Center... And all sorts of cool business functions that would need were we to survive in "The Real World of Modern Charismania." But here was Keith Wheeler, almost a brigand to the cause, telling us: "Throw it all away for the sake of the cross." Whatever would I do?

At this point in my journey, the Hermeneutics, Homiletics, Exegesis and the Church Polity would have me taking the trek down the path of a modern day Judas Iscariot. I would be more concerned with payroll and book-keeping than I would in actually loving people. I think this was the reason for my immense distrust of Keith. He was a lot like Rich Mullins, I thought. Oddly enough, Keith had met Rich Mullins down in Guatemala, when Rich was filming several projects for Fire by Nite and Teen Mania and making music videos following his big release from the Awesome God album. Keith invited Rich to a Christian Concert where a fella named Rich Mullins was going to be performing.

"I'll be there" Rich told him.

Keith then asked him his name.

"Rich." Rich Mullins said, and then said: "Keith, I promise you that I'll be at my concert."

Keith was so impressed with his humility, it stuck with him forever. If Rich was this humble, then what was stopping Keith from being this humble? And since I've known both of these guys, how could I embrace that humility as well? I needed to rethink everything. It was people that needed to be my mission... Not "Church Polity."

It was the intention of the heart that caused the arrow to strike the target... Not the theology of that target. The target was people. Their lives were the target. The arrow was love, and not accounting software. The goal was bringing people to Jesus, not in the "Hottest New Enriching Evangelism and Church Growth Package."

So I didn't leave, but adjusted myself instead. I stayed with Keith's program. We talked about modern day missiology and how it applied to the Book of Acts. Was there relevance? Was there a touchstone to move from? What were the ramifications of "Agape Love" vs. "Foolish Altruism"? He taught us that God was more interested in reaching all of us than we were in reaching all of the world.

But most importantly, Keith Wheeler modeled what it was to be a worshipper of God. I laughed one time at the tiny kneeling altar he had at his home until I noticed how worn out it was. The velvet cover had been worn away from where had placed his knees as he worshiped the Lord. This wasn't a decoration, this was a practicality. Keith fought the good fight on his knees, more than he did with his mouth.

Never once did I hear Keith bring up tithing and prosperity. What he did bring up were the words of Christ: "Blessed are the poor, for theirs is the kingdom of heaven." If ever I needed to know what "Real Christianity" was, I found it by the example set by Keith Wheeler. He made us memorize a map of the world, he made us run three miles, he made us memorize practical Bible verses, he made us preach on the streets.

And he did it all because he loved Jesus. Here was a man from Arkansas who came from wealth, who knew the Clinton family, and who was an Olympian hopeful in Pole-vaulting... But when Christ asked him to lay it all down at his feet: the money, the connections, the dream... Keith did it and never looked back. He took the verses literally: ""If anyone desires to come after Me, let him deny himself, and take up his cross daily, and follow Me." As well as "Blessed is the man whose strength is in You, Whose heart is set on pilgrimage."

Keith carries a large wooden cross around the world, spreading the love of Jesus to those he meets. "How beautiful upon the mountains are the feet of him that bring good news" comes to my mind every time I think of the man. He walks the world, carrying an actual cross, preaching with his actions and not his mouth.

He's been my lifelong mentor ever since. And I really do mean that. I love that guy with all the love I have in me. He's my personal hero... More so than anyone else could have been. And it's his theology that really cracks me up. It's so simple, it's perfect. I asked him two years ago about a theological issue I was having and his response to me was: "Well Paul... But is Jesus the focus?" Again I asked, more pointedly, and he answered: "Well. But does it center around Jesus?"

I got his point, and that phrase has become one of the most integral in my daily ministry.

The intention of the heart was at the intention of the heart of God.